D0002118

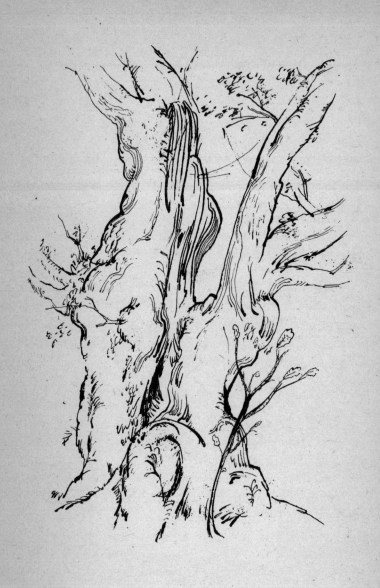

Isaac Bashevis Singer

Naftali the Storyteller and His Horse, Sus

and Other Stories

Pictures by Margot Zemach

A Yearling Book

Published by
Dell Publishing Co., Inc.
1 Dag Hammarskjold Plaza
New York, New York 10017

Of the eight stories in this book, six were translated from the Yiddish by my nephew, Joseph Singer, the son of my brother, master, and teacher, I. J. Singer. He is the Joshua mentioned in two of the stories together with my parents, my sister, Hindele, and my brother Moshe. "The Fools of Chelm and the Stupid Carp" was translated by Ruth Schachner Finkel and myself. "Dalfunka, Where the Rich Live Forever," I happened to write in English.

I dedicate these stories to the memory of my family and to all my readers, young and old, who contemplate the wonder of growing up and facing the riddle of life and love.

I.B.S.

Contents

Naftali the Storyteller and His Horse, Sus........13

Dalfunka, Where the Rich Live Forever.........39

The Lantuch 51

A Hanukkah Eve in Warsaw....................63

The Fools of Chelm and the Stupid Carp.........89

Lemel and Tzipa..............................99

The Cat Who Thought She Was a Dog and the
Dog Who Thought He Was a Cat............117

Growing Up 127

Naftali the Storyteller and His Horse, Sus

I

The father, Zelig, and the mother, Bryna, both complained that their son, Naftali, loved stories too much. He could never go to sleep unless his mother first told him a story. At times she had to tell him two or three stories before he would close his eyes. He always demanded: "Mama, more, more! . . ."

Fortunately, Bryna had heard many stories from her mother and grandmother. Zelig himself, a coachman, had many things to tell—about spirits who posed as passengers and imps who stole into stables at night and wove braids into the horses' tails and elflocks into their manes. The nicest story was about when Zelig had still been a young coachman.

One summer night Zelig was coming home from Lublin with an empty wagon. It just so happened that he hadn't picked up any passengers from Lublin to his hometown, Janów. He drove along a road that ran through a forest. There was a full moon. It cast silvery nets over the pine branches and strings of pearls over the bark of the tree trunks. Night birds cried. From time to time a wolf's howl was heard. In those days the Polish woods still swarmed with bears, wolves, foxes, martens, and many other wild beasts. That night Zelig was despondent. When his wagon was empty of passengers, his wallet was empty of money, and there wouldn't be enough for Bryna to prepare for the Sabbath.

Suddenly Zelig saw lying in the road a sack that appeared to be full of flour or ground sugar. Zelig stopped his horse and got down to take a look. A sack of flour or sugar would come in handy in a household.

Zelig untied the sack, opened it, took a lick, and decided that it was ground sugar. He lifted the sack, which was unusually heavy. Zelig was accustomed to carrying his passengers' baggage and he wondered why a sack of sugar should feel so heavy.

"It seems I didn't have enough to eat at the inn," Zelig thought. "And when you don't eat enough, you lose your strength."

He loaded the sack into the wagon. It was so heavy that he nearly strained himself.

He sat down on the driver's box and pulled on the reins, but the horse didn't move.

Zelig tugged harder and cried out, *"Wyszta!"* which in Polish means "Giddap!"

But even though the horse pulled with all his might, the wagon still wouldn't move forward.

"What's going on here?" Zelig wondered. "Can the sack be so heavy that the horse cannot pull it?"

This made no sense, for the horse had often drawn a wagonful of passengers along with their baggage.

"There is something here that's not as it should be," Zelig said to himself. He got down again, untied the sack, and took another lick. God in heaven, the sack was full of salt, not sugar!

Zelig stood there dumfounded. How could he have made such a mistake? He licked again, and again, and it was salt.

"Well, it's one of those nights!" Zelig mumbled to himself.

He decided to heave the sack off the wagon, since it was clear that evil spirits were toying with him. But by now the sack had become as heavy as if it were filled with lead. The horse turned his head backward and stared, as if curious as to what

was going on.

Suddenly Zelig heard laughter coming from inside the sack. Soon afterward the sack crumbled and out popped a creature with the eyes of a calf, the horns of a goat, and the wings of a bat. The creature said in a human voice, "You didn't lick sugar or salt but an imp's tail."

And with these words the imp burst into wild laughter and flew away.

Dozens of times Zelig the coachman told this

same story to Naftali but Naftali never grew tired of hearing it. He could picture it all—the forest, the night, the silver moon, the curious eye of the horse, the imp. Naftali asked all kinds of questions: Did the imp have a beard? Did it have feet? How did its tail look? Where did it fly off to?

Zelig couldn't answer all the questions. He had been too frightened at the time to notice the details. But to the last question Zelig replied, "He probably flew to beyond the Dark Regions, where people don't go and cattle don't stray, where the sky is copper, the earth iron, and where the evil forces live under roofs of petrified toadstools and in tunnels abandoned by moles."

II

Like all the children in town, Naftali rose early to go to cheder. He studied more diligently than the other children. Why? Because Naftali was eager to learn to read. He had seen older boys reading storybooks and he had been envious of them. How happy was one who could read a story from a book!

At six, Naftali was already able to read a book in Yiddish, and from then on he read every storybook he could get his hands on. Twice a year a bookseller named Reb Zebulun visited Janów, and among the other books in the sack he carried over his shoulder were some storybooks. They cost two groshen a copy, and although Naftali got only two groshen a week allowance from his father, he saved up enough to buy a number of storybooks each season. He also read the stories in his mother's Yiddish Pentateuch and in her books of morals.

When Naftali grew older, his father began to teach him how to handle horses. It was the custom in those days for a son to take over his father's livelihood. Naftali loved horses very much but he wasn't anxious to become a coachman driving passengers from Janów to Lublin and from Lublin to Janów. He wanted to become a bookseller with a sackful of storybooks.

His mother said to him, "What's so good about being a bookseller? From toting the sack day in day out, your back becomes bent, and from all the walking, your legs swell."

Naftali knew that his mother was right and he thought a lot about what he would do when he grew up. Suddenly he came up with a plan that seemed to him both wise and simple. He would get himself a horse and wagon, and instead of carrying the books on his back, he would carry them in the wagon.

His father, Zelig, said, "A bookseller doesn't make enough to support himself, his family, and a horse besides."

"For me it will be enough."

One time when Reb Zebulun the bookseller came to town, Naftali had a talk with him. He asked him where he got the storybooks and who wrote them. The bookseller told him that in Lublin there was a printer who printed these books, and in Warsaw and Vilna there were writers who wrote them. Reb Zebulun said that he could sell many more storybooks, but he lacked the strength to walk to all the towns and villages, and it didn't pay him to do so.

Reb Zebulun said, "I'm liable to come to a town where there are only two or three children who want to read storybooks. It doesn't pay me to walk there for the few groshen I might earn nor does it pay me to keep a horse or hire a wagon."

"What do these children do without storybooks?" Naftali asked. And Reb Zebulun replied, "They have to make do. Storybooks aren't bread. You can live without them."

"I couldn't live without them," Naftali said.

During this conversation Naftali also asked where the writers got all these stories and Reb Zebulun said, "First of all, many unusual things happen in the world. A day doesn't go by without some rare event happening. Besides, there are writers who make up such stories."

"They make them up?" Naftali asked in amazement. "If that is so, then they are liars."

"They are not liars," Reb Zebulun replied. "The human brain really can't make up a thing. At times

I read a story that seems to me completely unbelievable, but I come to some place and I hear that such a thing actually happened. The brain is created by God, and human thoughts and fantasies are also God's works. Even dreams come from God. If a thing doesn't happen today, it might easily happen tomorrow. If not in one country, then in another. There are endless worlds and what doesn't happen on earth can happen in another world. Whoever has eyes that see and ears that hear absorbs enough stories to last a lifetime and to tell to his children and grandchildren."

That's what old Reb Zebulun said, and Naftali listened to his words agape.

Finally, Naftali said, "When I grow up, I'll travel to all the cities, towns, and villages, and I'll sell storybooks everywhere, whether it pays me or not."

Naftali had decided on something else too—to become a writer of storybooks. He knew full well that for this you had to study, and with all his heart he determined to learn. He also began to listen more closely to what people said, to what stories they told, and to how they told them. Each person had his or her own manner of speaking. Reb Zebulun told Naftali, "When a day passes, it is no longer there. What remains of it? Nothing more than a story. If stories weren't told or books weren't written, man would live like beasts, only for the day."

Reb Zebulun said, "Today we live, but by tomor-

row today will be a story. The whole world, all
human life, is one long story."

III

Ten years went by. Naftali was now a young man.
He grew up tall, slim, fair-skinned, with black hair
and blue eyes. He had learned a lot at the study-
house and in the yeshiva and he was also an expert
horseman. Zelig's mare had borne a colt and Naftali pastured and raised it. He called him Sus. Sus
was a playful colt. In the summer he liked to roll
in the grass. He whinnied like the tinkling sound
of a bell. Sometimes, when Naftali washed and
curried him and tickled his neck, Sus burst out in
a sound that resembled laughter. Naftali rode him
bareback like a Cossack. When Naftali passed the
marketplace astride Sus, the town girls ran to the
windows to look out.

After a while Naftali built himself a wagon. He
ordered the wheels from Leib the blacksmith. Naftali loaded the wagon with all the storybooks he
had collected during the years and he rode with his
horse and his goods to the nearby towns. Naftali
bought a whip, but he swore solemnly to himself
that he would never use it. Sus didn't need to be

whipped or even to have the whip waved at him.
He pulled the light wagonful of books eagerly and
easily. Naftali seldom sat on the box but walked
alongside his horse and told him stories. Sus
cocked his ears when Naftali spoke to him and
Naftali was sure that Sus understood him. At
times, when Naftali asked Sus whether he had
liked a story, Sus whinnied, stomped his foot on
the ground, or licked Naftali's ear with his tongue
as if he meant to say, "Yes, I understand . . ."

Reb Zebulun had told him that animals live only for the day, but Naftali was convinced that animals have a memory too. Sus often remembered the road better than he, Naftali, did. Naftali had heard the story of a dog whose masters had lost him on a distant journey and months after they had come home without their beloved pet, he showed up. The dog crossed half of Poland to come back to his owners. Naftali had heard a similar story about a cat. The fact that pigeons fly back to their coops from very far away was known throughout the world. In those days, they were often used to deliver letters. Some people said this was memory, others called it instinct. But what did it matter what it was called? Animals didn't live for the day only.

Naftali rode from town to town; he often stopped in villages and sold his storybooks. The children everywhere loved Naftali and his horse, Sus. They brought all kinds of good things from home for Sus—potato peels, turnips, and pieces of sugar—and each time Sus got something to eat he waved his tail and shook his head, which meant "Thank you."

Not all the children were able to study and learn to read, and Naftali would gather a number of young children, seat them in the wagon, and tell them a story, sometimes a real one and sometimes a made-up one.

Wherever he went, Naftali heard all kinds of

tales—of demons, hobgoblins, windmills, giants, dwarfs, kings, princes, and princesses. He would tell a story nicely, with all the details, and the children never grew tired of listening to him. Even grownups came to listen. Often the grownups invited Naftali home for a meal or a place to sleep. They also liked to feed Sus.

When a person does his work not only for money but out of love, he brings out the love in others. When a child couldn't afford a book, Naftali gave it to him free. Soon Naftali became well known throughout the region. Eventually, he came to Lublin.

In Lublin, Naftali heard many astonishing stories. He met a giant seven feet tall who traveled with a circus and a troupe of midgets. At the circus Naftali saw horses who danced to music, as well as dancing bears. One trickster swallowed a knife and spat it out again, another did a somersault on a high wire, a third flew in the air from one trapeze to another. A girl stood on a horse's back while it raced round and round the circus ring. Naftali struck up an easy friendship with the circus people and he listened to their many interesting stories. They told of fakirs in India who could walk barefoot over burning coals. Others let themselves be buried alive, and after they were dug out several days later, they were healthy and well. Naftali heard astonishing stories about sorcerers and miracle workers who could read minds and predict the future. He met an old man who had walked from Lublin to the Land of Israel, then back again. The old man told Naftali about cabalists who lived in caves behind Jerusalem, fasted from one Sabbath to the next, and learned the secrets of God, the angels, the seraphim, the cherubim, and the holy beasts.

The world was full of wonders and Naftali had the urge to write them down and spread them far and wide over all the cities, towns, and villages.

In Lublin, Naftali went to the bookstores and bought storybooks, but he soon saw that there weren't enough storybooks to be had. The storekeepers said that it didn't pay the printers to print them since they brought in so little money. But could everything be measured by money? There were children and even grownups everywhere who yearned to hear stories and Naftali decided to tell all that he had heard. He himself hungered for stories and could never get enough of them.

IV

More years passed. Naftali's parents were no longer living. Many girls had fallen in love with Naftali and wanted to marry him, but he knew that from telling stories and selling storybooks he could not support a family. Besides, he had become used to wandering. How many stories could he hear or tell living in one town? He therefore decided to stay on the road. Horses normally live some twenty-odd years, but Sus was one of those rare horses who live a long time. However, no one lives forever. At forty Sus began to show signs of old age. He seldom galloped now, nor were his eyes as good as they once were. Naftali was already gray himself and the children called him Grandpa.

One time Naftali was told that on the road between Lublin and Warsaw lay an estate where all booksellers came, since the owner was very fond of reading and hearing stories. Naftali asked the way and he was given directions to get there. One spring day he came to the estate. Everything that had been said turned out to be true. The owner of the estate, Reb Falik, gave him a warm welcome and bought many books from him. The children in the nearby town had already heard about Naftali the storyteller and they snatched up all the storybooks he had brought with him. Reb Falik had many horses grazing and when they saw Sus they accepted him as one of their own. Sus promptly began to chew the grass where many yellow flowers grew and Naftali told Reb Falik one story after another. The weather was warm, birds sang, twittered, and trilled, each in its own voice.

The estate contained a tract of forest where old

oaks grew. Some of the oaks were so thick they had
to be hundreds of years old. Naftali was particu-
larly taken by one oak standing in the center of a
meadow. It was the thickest oak Naftali had ever
seen in his life. Its roots were spread over a wide
area and you could tell that they ran deep. The
crown of the oak spread far and wide, and it cast
a huge shadow. When Naftali saw this giant oak,
which had to be older than all the oaks in the
region, it occurred to him: "What a shame an oak
hasn't a mouth to tell stories with!"

This oak had lived through many generations.
It may have gone back to the times when idol wor-
shippers still lived in Poland. It surely knew the
time when the Jews had come to Poland from the
German states where they had been persecuted and
the Polish king, Kazimierz I, had opened the gates
of the land to them. Naftali suddenly realized that
he was tired of wandering. He now envied the oak
for standing so long in one place, deeply rooted in
God's earth. For the first time in his life Naftali
got the urge to settle down in one place. He also
thought of his horse. Sus was undoubtedly tired
of trekking over the roads. It would do him good
to get some rest in the few years left him.

Just as Naftali stood there thinking these
thoughts, the owner of the estate, Reb Falik, came
along in a buggy. He stopped the buggy near Naftali and said, "I see you're completely lost in
thought. Tell me what you're thinking."

At first Naftali wanted to tell Reb Falik that many kinds of foolish notions ran through the human mind and that not all of them could be described. But after a while he thought, "Why not tell him the truth?"

Reb Falik seemed a goodhearted man. He had a silver-white beard and eyes that expressed the wisdom and goodness that sometimes come with age. Naftali said, "If you have the patience, I'll tell you."

"Yes, I have the patience. Take a seat in the buggy. I'm going for a drive and I want to hear what a man who is famous for his storytelling thinks about."

Naftali sat down in the buggy. The horses hitched to the buggy walked slowly and Naftali told Reb Falik the story of his life, as well as what his thoughts were when he saw the giant oak. He told him everything, kept nothing back.

When Naftali finished, Reb Falik said, "My dear Naftali, I can easily fulfill all your wishes and fantasies. I am, as you know, an old man. My wife died some time ago. My children live in the big cities. I love to hear stories and I also have lots of stories to tell. If you like, I'll let you build a house in the shade of the oak and you can stay there as long as I live and as long as you live. I'll have a stable built for your horse near the house and you'll both live out your lives in peace. Yes, you are right. You cannot wander forever. There comes a time when every person wants to settle in one place and drink in all the charms that the place has to offer."

When Naftali heard these words, a great joy came over him. He thanked Reb Falik again and again, but Reb Falik said, "You need not thank me so much. I have many peasants and servants here, but I don't have a single person I can talk to. We'll be friends and we'll tell each other lots of stories. What's life, after all? The future isn't here yet and you cannot foresee what it will bring. The present is only a moment and the past is one long story. Those who don't tell stories and don't hear stories live only for that moment, and that isn't enough."

V

Reb Falik's promise wasn't merely words. The very next day he ordered his people to build a house for Naftali the storyteller. There was no shortage of lumber or of craftsmen on the estate. When Naftali saw the plans for the house, he grew disturbed. He needed only a small house for himself and a stable for Sus. But the plans called for a big house with many rooms. Naftali asked Reb Falik why such a big house was being built for him, and Reb Falik replied, "You will need it."

"What for?" Naftali asked.

Gradually, the secret came out. During his lifetime Reb Falik had accumulated many books, so many that he couldn't find room for them in his own big house and many books had to be stored in the cellar and in the attic. Besides, in his talks with Reb Falik, Naftali had said that he had many of his own stories and stories told him by others written down on paper and that he had collected a chestful of manuscripts, but he hadn't been able to have these stories printed, for the printers in Lublin and in the other big cities demanded a lot of money to print them and the number of buyers of storybooks in Poland wasn't large enough to cover such expenses.

Alongside Naftali's house, Reb Falik had a print shop built. He ordered crates of type from Lublin (in those days there was no such thing as a typesetting machine) as well as a hand press. From now on Naftali would have the opportunity to set and print his own storybooks. When he learned what Reb Falik was doing for him, Naftali couldn't believe his ears. He said, "Of all the stories I have ever heard or told, for me this will be by far the nicest."

That very summer everything was ready—the house, the library, the print shop. Winter came early. Right after Succoth the rains began, followed by snow. In winter there is little to do on an estate. The peasants sat in their huts and warmed themselves by their stoves or they went to the tavern. Reb Falik and Naftali spent lots of time together. Reb Falik himself was a treasure trove of stories. He had met many famous squires. In his time he had visited the fairs in Danzig, Leipzig, and Amsterdam. He had even made a trip to the Holy Land and had seen the Western Wall, the Cave of Machpelah, and Rachel's Tomb. Red Felik told many tales and Naftali wrote them down.

Sus's stable was too big for one horse. Reb Falik had a number of old horses on his estate that could no longer work so Sus wasn't alone. At times, when Naftali came into the stable to visit his beloved Sus, he saw him bowing his head against the horse on his left or his right, and it seemed to Naftali that Sus was listening to stories told him by the other horses or silently telling his own horsy story. It's true that horses cannot speak, but God's creatures can make themselves understood without words.

That winter Naftali wrote many stories—his own and those he heard from Reb Falik. He set them in type and printed them on his hand press. At times, when the sun shone over the silvery snow, Naftali hitched Sus and another horse to a sleigh and made a trip through the nearby towns to sell his storybooks or give them away to those who couldn't afford to buy them. Sometimes Reb Falik went along with him. They slept at inns and spent time with merchants, landowners, and Hasi-

dim on their way to visit their rabbis' courts. Each
one had a story to tell and Naftali either wrote
them down or fixed them in his memory.

The winter passed and Naftali couldn't remember how. On Passover, Reb Falik's sons, daughters,
and grandchildren came to celebrate the holiday
at the estate, and again Naftali heard wondrous
tales of Warsaw, Cracow, and even of Berlin, Paris,
and London. The kings waged wars, but scientists
made all kinds of discoveries and inventions.
Astronomers discovered stars, planets, comets.
Archaeologists dug out ruins of ancient cities.
Chemists found new elements. In all the countries,
tracks were being laid for railroad trains. Mu-
seums, libraries, and theaters were being built.
Historians uncovered writings from generations
past. The writers in every land described the life
and the people among whom they dwelled. Man-
kind could not and would not forget its past. The
history of the world grew ever richer in detail.

That spring something happened that Naftali
had been expecting and, therefore, dreading. Sus
became sick and stopped grazing. The sun shone
outside, and Naftali led Sus out to pasture where
the fresh green grass and many flowers sprouted.
Sus sat down in the sunshine, looked at the grass
and the flowers, but no longer grazed. A stillness
shone out from his eyes, the tranquillity of a creature that has lived out its years and is ready to end
its story on earth.

One afternoon, when Naftali went out to check on his beloved Sus, he saw that Sus was dead. Naftali couldn't hold back his tears. Sus had been a part of his life.

Naftali dug a grave for Sus not far from the old oak where Sus had died, and he buried him there. As a marker over the grave, he thrust into the ground the whip that he had never used. Its handle was made of oak.

Oddly enough, several weeks later Naftali noticed that the whip had turned into a sapling. The handle had put down roots into the earth where Sus lay and it began to sprout leaves. A tree grew over Sus, a new oak which drew sustenance from Sus's body. In time young branches grew out of the tree and birds sang upon them and built their nests there. Naftali could hardly bring himself to believe that this old dried-out stick had possessed enough life within it to grow and blossom. Naftali considered it a miracle. When the tree grew thicker, Naftali carved Sus's name into the bark along with the dates of his birth and death.

Yes, individual creatures die, but this doesn't end the story of the world. The whole earth, all the stars, all the planets, all the comets represent within them one divine history, one source of life, one endless and wondrous story that only God knows in its entirety.

A few years afterward, Reb Falik died, and years later, Naftali the storyteller died. By then he was

famous for his storybooks not only throughout
Poland but in other countries as well. Before his
death Naftali asked that he be buried beneath the
young oak that had grown over Sus's grave and
whose branches touched the old oak. On Naftali's
tombstone were carved these words from the Scriptures:

> LOVELY AND PLEASANT IN THEIR LIVES,
> AND IN THEIR DEATH
> THEY WERE NOT DIVIDED

Dalfunka, Where the Rich Live Forever

It happened in Chelm, a city of fools. Where else could it have happened? On a winter morning in the community house Gronam Ox, the wisest man of Chelm, and his five sages, Dopey Lekisch, Zeinvel Ninny, Treitel Fool, Sender Donkey, and Shmendrick Numskull sat at a long table. All six looked tired and had red eyes from lack of sleep. For seven days and nights they had been thinking about a problem which they could not solve. The treasury of the city of Chelm was empty. For many weeks Gronam Ox and his sages had not received their salaries.

Even though it was not Hanukkah, Shlemiel the beadle sat at the other end of the table playing dreidel by himself. Suddenly the door opened and Zalman Typpesh entered. He was the richest man in Chelm. He had a long white beard. When they saw Zalman Typpesh, Gronam and the sages looked up in surprise. Zalman Typpesh never paid a visit to the community house because they levied high taxes on him.

"Good morning, Gronam Ox. Good morning, sages," Zalman Typpesh greeted them solemnly.

"A good morning to you, Zalman Typpesh," all of them answered in accord. "What made you pay such an early visit?"

"I came to ask your advice," Zalman Typpesh said. "If it is good I will pay the treasury two thousand gold pieces."

"What sort of advice?" Gronam Ox asked.

"You all know I have just turned eighty. You also know that no man lives forever. But I, Zalman Typpesh, wish to live forever. I would like forever to eat blintzes with sour cream, drink tea with jam, coffee with chicory, forever smoke my long pipe. To make it short, I want to live forever."

"Live forever!" exclaimed Gronam Ox and his five sages. "How is this possible?"

"This is the reason I came to you," Zelman said. "If you will tell me how to live forever, you will get what I just promised." Saying these words, Zalman Typpesh took out a bag filled with gold coins and poured them on the table.

When Gronam and his sages saw the pile of gold, they began to murmur. Zalman Typpesh was known as a miser. Gronam Ox immediately put his index finger on his forehead in order think hard. The other sages did the same thing. After long thought, Gronam Ox said, "You know well that Chelm is the wisest city in the world and I, Gronam Ox, am the wisest man in Chelm, which means that I am the wisest man in the universe. But just the same, I cannot give you the kind of advice you desire. No man can live forever. Even I, Gronam Ox, won't live forever."

"Even Methuselah did not live forever," Dopey Lekisch chimed in.

"Even King Solomon did not live forever," Zein-vel Ninny added.

"'Even our rabbi is not going to live forever," Treitel Fool pronounced.

"Even a lion does not live forever," Sender Donkey remarked.

"Even an elephant does not live forever," Shmendrick Numskull said.

"All this is true, but I, Zalman Typpesh, decided that I must live forever. If you won't advise me how to do it, you won't get a penny."

Gronam Ox was about to say that he was sorry, but at that moment Shlemiel the beadle stuck out

his tongue and placed his thumb on the tip of his
nose as a sign that he wanted to speak.

"What do you want to say, Shlemiel?" Gronam
Ox asked.

"I found a way," Shlemiel said.

"You found a way?" Gronam Ox asked in aston-
ishment.

"Yes, my lord. The thing is like this. Last week I

had nothing to do all day long and I started to look over the records of our Chelm suburbs. Among others I glanced through the records of our suburb Dalfunka."

"Dalfunka, where all the paupers and beggars of Chelm live?" Gronam Ox asked.

"Yes, Dalfunka," Shlemiel said. "As you know, we have in our books the names of all those who were born and died in the last three hundred years. When I went through the list of all who died in Dalfunka, I realized that no rich man ever died there. This means that the rich in Dalfunka live forever. My advice therefore is that Zalman Typpesh should buy a house in Dalfunka, settle there, and never die. As simple as that."

Gronam Ox opened his mouth and stared agape. "Shlemiel, you gave the right advice. But how is this possible? Are you cleverer than I am?"

"No one is cleverer than you, Gronam Ox," the five sages sang out in chorus.

"My only explanation is that since you have been sitting so many years near us, a part of our wisdom spilled over on you," said Gronam Ox.

"True," the five sages agreed.

Dopey Lekisch added, "Even a horse would become wise if it stayed with us so long."

"Zalman, you got good advice. Now give us the two thousand gold coins," Gronam Ox suggested.

"Before I give you so much money, I must be sure that the advice is right," Zalman Typpesh answered. "I will give you an advance of ten gold coins now, and after I have moved to Dalfunka and have lived forever, I will pay the balance."

"We cannot wait that long," Gronam Ox protested. "We need the payment right now."

"Either take the ten gold coins or you will receive nothing," Zalman Typpesh insisted.

For a long while Gronam Ox and his sages haggled with Zalman Typpesh, but as always Zalman Typpesh prevailed. He gave Gronam Ox the ten gold coins and left.

For five years Zalman Typpesh lived in Dalfunka, ate blintzes with sour cream, drank tea with jam, coffee with chickory, smoked his long pipe, and did not die. Gronam Ox often asked for the balance, but Zalman Typpesh always had the same answer: "First let me live forever and then I will pay." It seemed that Zalman Typpesh was right in not paying beforehand, because one day in the sixth year he became sick and died.

When Gronam Ox heard the bad news he immediately called for the sages and they pondered seven days and seven nights why Zalman Typpesh had died. Again Shlemiel found the explanation. For five years Zalman did no business because one could not earn any money in Dalfunka. Instead, he spent a fortune on such luxuries as sour cream, coffee, tobacco, chickory. He most probably became poor and so he died like all the other poor people.

"To live forever in Dalfunka one must be as rich as Rothschild," Shlemiel said.

Gronam Ox and the five sages again admired Shlemiel's sharp mind. Gronam Ox promptly dispatched letters to the Rothschilds inviting them to come speedily to Dalfunka and begin to live forever. But months passed and the Rothschilds did not arrive. This time Gronam Ox discovered the reason himself. He said, "The rich are so stingy that they would rather die cheaply in London, Paris, and Vienna than live forever in Dalfunka at a higher cost."

"So what should we do now?" the sages asked.

"We must get rich ourselves."

"How?" the sages asked.

"Of course, by levying taxes on the paupers of Chelm," Gronam Ox replied.

Shlemiel made the usual sign that he wanted to speak. He wanted to say that, according to his latest figures, even the Rothschilds were not rich enough to live forever in Dalfunka, but Gronam Ox said, "Shlemiel, everything is crystal clear. We don't need your advice any more. Keep quiet."

"Be silent," Dopey Lekisch chimed in.

"You are only a beadle, not a sage," Zeinvel Ninny shouted.

"Not even half a sage," Treitel Fool screamed.

"And you will never live forever," Sender Donkey hollered.

"Not even a half of forever," Shmendrick Num-skull yelled.

Since he was forbidden to talk and he had nothing else to do, Shlemiel took out his dreidel and began to play by himself. While the dreidel spun, Shlemiel was muttering, "If it falls to the right, I lose, and if it falls to the left, you win."

The Lantuch

In the summers, my Aunt Yentl liked to tell stories on the Sabbath after the main meal, when my Uncle Joseph lay down for a nap. My aunt would take a seat on the bench in front of the house, and the cat, Dvosha, would join her. On the Sabbaths the cat would be given the remnants of the Sabbath meal—scraps of meat and fish. Dvosha would plant herself at my aunt's feet; she liked to hear my aunt tell stories. From the way she cocked her ears and narrowed her eyes, green as gooseberries,

it was apparent she understood what my aunt was saying.

For the Sabbath, my aunt wore a dress sewn with arabesques and a bonnet with glass beads, festooned with green, red, and blue ribbons. Presently, my mother came out and two of our female neighbors, Riva and Sheindel. I was the last to emerge and I took a seat on a footstool. Beside the

fact that I liked to listen to my Aunt Yentl's stories,
sooner or later I would get from her the Sabbath
fruit—an apple, a pear, plums. Sometimes she
would give me a Sabbath cookie baked with cin-
namon and raisins. She always said the same thing
when she gave it to me, "It'll give you the strength
to study."

This time the conversation centered on a house
demon or a sprite called a lantuch. Aunt Yentl
liked to talk about spirits, demons, and hobgoblins,
and I heard her say, "A lantuch? Yes, there is such
a spirit as a lantuch. These days people don't believe in such things, but in my time they knew that
everything can't be explained away with reason.
The world is full of secrets. A lantuch is an imp,
but he's not malicious. He causes no harm. On the
contrary, he tries to help the members of the household all he can. He is like a part of the family.
Usually he is invisible, but it sometimes happens
that you can see him. Where do they live? Sometimes in a cellar, sometimes in a woodshed, sometimes behind the stove along with the cricket.
Lantuchs love crickets. They bring them food and
they understand their language."

"Aunt Yentl, when I grow up I'll learn the language of crickets," I piped up.

Aunt Yentl smiled with every wrinkle in her
face. "My child, this isn't a language that can be
learned. Only King Solomon knew the language of
beasts. He could talk with the lions, the bears, the

wolves, and with all the birds too. But let's get back
to the lantuch. There was a lantuch at my parents'
house. In the summers he lived in the woodshed,
and in the winters behind the stove. We didn't see
him, but sometimes we heard him. One time when
my sister Keila sneezed, he said, 'God bless you!'
We all heard it. The lantuch loved us all, but he
loved my sister Keila most of all. When Keila married and went to live in Lublin with her in-laws—
I was only a girl of eight then—the lantuch came
to her on her last night home to say goodbye. In
the middle of the night Keila heard a rustle and
the door opened by itself.

"The lantuch came up to Keila's bed and said in
rhyme:

> " '*Wash basin,*
> *soak basin,*
> *meat cleaver*
> *kugel-eater*
> *I'll fret*
> *And you won't forget.'*

"Keila became so frightened that she lost her
tongue. He kissed her forehead, and soon after he
left. For a long time Keila lay there in a daze, then
she lit a candle. Keila was very fond of almond
cake. When my mother, may she rest in peace,
baked almond cake for Simchat Torah or Purim,
Keila would nibble half of it. Anyway, she lit the

candle and on her blanket lay an almond cake still warm from the oven. She started to cry and we all came running in to her. I saw the almond cake with my own eyes. Where the lantuch got it from, I haven't the slightest idea. Maybe some housewife happened to bake almond cakes and he pinched one, or maybe they know how to bake them themselves. Keila didn't eat the cake, but she put it away some place, and it grew hard as a stone.

"In our town of Janów there was a teacher who had a sick wife and an only daughter who had been blind from birth. All of a sudden the teacher died and the two women were left all alone and helpless. There was talk in town of putting the two women in the poorhouse, but who wants to go to a poorhouse? The paupers there lay on straw pallets right on the bare floor and the food wasn't good either. When the attendant came to take the mother and daughter to the poorhouse, they both began to lament: 'Rather than rot away in the poorhouse we'd sooner die!'

"You can't force anyone to go to the poorhouse. The attendant thought, 'The husband probably left them a few gulden, and so long as they still have some bread, they'll put on airs. When they get hungry enough, they'll thank God there is such a place as the poorhouse.'

"Days went by and weeks, and the mother and daughter still didn't give in. The town grew curious —what were they up to? The mother was bedridden and the daughter blind. There are blind people who can get around, but the teacher's daughter —Tzirel was her name—never strayed beyond her own courtyard. I can see her now: reddish hair, a glowing face, trim limbs. Her eyes were blue and appeared healthy, but she couldn't see a thing. People began to wonder if maybe the mother and daughter had more money than had been assumed, but that couldn't be. First of all, the teacher had been poor, and second, neither the mother nor the daughter ever left the house. Neither of them was ever seen in any store. Then where did they get the food, even if they did have the money?

"My dear people, there was a lantuch in their house, and when he saw that the breadwinner was gone and the women had been left penniless and without a stitch to their backs, he assumed the burden himself. You're laughing? It's nothing to laugh at. He brought them everything they needed —bread, sugar, herring. He did it all at night. One time a youth walked by their house in the middle of the night and he heard wood being chopped in the yard. He grew suspicious. Who would be chopping wood in the middle of the night? He opened the gate to the courtyard and saw an ax swinging and chips flying, but there was no one there. It was the lantuch chopping wood for the winter. The next day, when the youth revealed what he had seen, people laughed at him. 'You probably dreamed it,' they said. But it was true.

"A few weeks later, a shipping agent came back from Lublin, also in the middle of the night. He walked past a well and he saw the rope descending into the water and a pailful of water coming up. But there was no one around. He promptly realized that this was the work of *that* band—the creatures of the night. But the shipping agent—Meir David was his name—was a strong person and not easily frightened. He took hold of his ritual fringes, quietly recited 'Hear O Israel,' and stopped to see what would happen next. After the unseen one had drawn one pail of water, he drew a second, and then the two pails began to be borne along as if an invisible water carrier were carrying them on a yoke. Meir David followed the pails of water to where the widow and her blind daughter lived. The next day the shipping agent went to the rabbi and told him what his eyes had seen. This Meir David was an honest man and not one to make up things. A fuss erupted in town. The rabbi summoned the widow and her daughter to him, but the widow was too sick to walk. She couldn't talk either. Soon after, she died.

"The blind daughter said to the rabbi, 'Someone provides for us, but who it is I do not know. It must be an angel from heaven.'

"No, it wasn't any angel but the lantuch. After the mother died, the daughter sold the house and went to live with relatives in Galicia."

"The lantuch didn't go along?" our neighbor Riva asked.

"Who knows? As a rule, they don't stir from the house," Aunt Yentl said.

"Do they live forever?" Sheindel asked.

"No one lives forever," Aunt Yentl replied.

It grew silent. I looked at the cat; she had fallen asleep.

Aunt Yentl glanced at me. "I'll get you the Sabbath fruit now. If a young man wants to study the Torah, he must keep up his strength."

And she brought me a Sabbath cookie and three plums.

A Hanukkah Eve in Warsaw

I

For two weeks now Warsaw—and perhaps all
Poland—had lain in the grip of a cold spell the
likes of which hadn't been seen in years. But I, a
child not yet seven, kept going to cheder early
each morning. We—my parents, my older brother
Joshua, my sister Hindele, my younger brother
Moshe, and I—lived at 10 Krochmalna Street and
the cheder was located at 5 Grzybowska Street. In
the mornings, an assistant to the teacher came to
take me to cheder, and he brought me home again

in the evenings. To keep me from freezing on the way, Mother wrapped me in two woolen vests, two pairs of socks, and gloves. She stuck a hood on my head which covered my red hair and earlocks; when I looked in the mirror I couldn't recognize myself and stuck my tongue out at the stranger.

The long winter night passed full of dreams. Now I dreamed I was an emperor, and now a beggar. An old crone of a gypsy snatched me and locked me in a cellar. I also dreamed that it was summer and that I was strolling with Shosha, the daughter of our neighbor Bashele, in a garden full of blooming flowers and singing birds. I sailed a boat on the Vistula but soon pirates captured me and spirited me off to Madagascar to be sold into slavery. My dreams blended with my fantasies and with the tales I had heard from my mother or read in storybooks.

That winter morning was a cold but sunny one. The sky above the rooftops loomed a light blue. Although our oven was heated with wood and coal, frost patterns had formed on our windows overnight. They resembled trees, not those common to Poland, but rather the date palms and fig and carob trees the Bible said grew in the Land of Israel.

Normally, I stayed at the cheder until nightfall, but that day was the eve of Hanukkah and I was scheduled to come home earlier than usual. I liked Hanukkah—the only holiday that came in the winter. In the evening, right after services, Father would bless the Hanukkah candles, Mother would fry potato pancakes, I would get a tin dreidel and money for the holiday. I could hardly wait to get home.

Before I left the house, Mother gave me a paper bag containing bread and butter, cheese, and an apple. This was to be my second breakfast. The assistant teacher took my hand and led me down the stairs into the street. Mother warned him not to let go of me. In such a large city a child could easily get lost. The streets were filled with sleighs and I was liable to be run over, God forbid. I was ashamed that my mother was such a worrier. She came from a small town and provincial people imagined all kinds of dangers in the big city. I had come to Warsaw when I was three and I considered myself a city boy. I could have gone to cheder by myself; I didn't have to be escorted there. I envied the other children my age who went to cheder alone. It seemed to me they laughed at me for being escorted like a baby.

God in heaven, how different the street looked today all covered by the fresh snow that had fallen overnight! The sleighs and pedestrians hadn't yet managed to trample it, and it glared beneath the sun, reflecting dazzling crystals of every color of the rainbow. One solitary tree grew on our street and its naked branches were covered with frost. They reminded me of the arms of a huge Hanukkah candelabrum. Sleighs rode by with bells on horses' collars jingling. The animals' nostrils exuded steam. Cushions of snow lay on roofs and balconies. The whole world had turned white, rich and dreamlike.

II

Coming to cheder was for me a daily trial. The other pupils quickly made friends with one another. They conducted all kinds of secret business transactions among themselves. One boy gave another a silver button and got a gold button in exchange. Quietly, so that the teacher wouldn't see, they traded pencils, pens, and sometimes chocolates and cookies they brought from home. Most of the students were sons of storekeepers or factory owners and were already little businessmen themselves. Their parents lived in the wealthier streets. Some of the students brought a different toy to cheder each day—lead soldiers, whistles, trumpets. One boy had a pen with a peephole. When you looked into it you saw Cracow. Another boy had a music box. When you turned the key it played a tune. One boy had a real watch. Most of them had black hair, and some were

blond, but no one in the cheder besides me had hair
as red as fire. Nor did anyone else wear such long
earlocks. I was a rabbi's son and my parents
dressed me in the old-fashioned style. I had been
raised in Warsaw, but I looked like a yokel. The
boys laughed at me and my small town costumes.
They even mocked the way I pronounced some
words in Yiddish. Besides, they couldn't do any
trading with me. I brought nothing to cheder except my Pentateuch.

I always felt ashamed when I came to cheder,
and I often prayed to God to let me grow up faster
so that I could be through with being a child. But
I had some satisfaction too. All children love to
hear stories and I had acquired the reputation of a
storyteller. I was also able to add my own fantasies
to the stories we read in the Pentateuch. At Hanukkah time the teacher studied with us the section
that dealt with Joseph and his brothers. I retained
the meaning of the Hebrew words better than
many of the other children, and I repeated the tale
as if I had been there in person. Joseph's dreams
became my dreams. The brothers envied me and
sold me into slavery to the Ishmaelites, who in
turn sold me to the Egyptians. Potiphar had me imprisoned, and later I became viceroy to Pharaoh.
Jacob, Joseph, the other tribes, Laban, Rachel,
Leah, Bilhah, Zilpah were all as close and familiar
to me as my own mother and father, as our neighbor Bashele and her daughter, Shosha, with whom

I carried on an unspoken love affair. As I sat in cheder over the Pentateuch, I yearned for her and her childish words, which held a thousand delights for me . . .

By three o'clock we had concluded our portion and the teacher, Reb Moshe Yitzchok, a patriarch of eighty, put down the pointer and the hare's leg with the thong that he used to whip bad pupils, and told us to go home.

The assistant teacher came up to me and began, with hesitation, "You always say that you could find your way home by yourself. Is this true?"

"Yes, it's true."

"You wouldn't get lost?"

"Lost? I could get home in the middle of the night!"

"I've got something to do and I don't have the time to take you home. Can I trust you to get home by yourself?"

"Yes, yes . . ."

"You won't tell your parents?"

"Tell? No, never!"

"Is that a promise?"

"I swear it on my ritual fringes."

"You don't have to swear on your ritual fringes."

"I wouldn't say anything even if they should kill me."

"Well, all right. Go straight home and don't stop along the way. You'll tell them I took you to the gate of your house."

"Yes."

The assistant teacher helped me put on my overcoat, the hood, the gloves, the galoshes. The other boys laughed and made fun of me. They called me a sissy, a mama's boy, a little rabbi, a spoiled brat. One of them showed me his tongue, another made the sign of the fig. A third said, "He is Joseph from the Bible. His father will make him a coat of many colors . . ."

III

I wanted to boast to the boys that I was going home all by myself, but the assistant teacher apparently guessed my intentions, for he put his finger to his lips.

I went out into the street and for the first time I felt like a grownup. How short the days were in winter! It was just a quarter past three but the sky was already a dusky blue. Several cheder boys were sliding on the frozen gutter, trying to make the figure called "little shoemaker." When they saw me walking alone, they began to yell and make faces as if about to chase me. One of them threw a snowball at me. I moved away from them quickly. They only waited for a chance to start a fight and show off their strength. On Gnoyna Street I stopped in front of a shop window. Although the store belonged to a Jew, it sold the globes, bells, lights, and spangles Gentiles drape on Christmas trees. A man holding a long pole lit the gas street lights. Women sat in doorways, on boxes and on footstools, hawking their wares—potato cakes, hot chick-peas, hot lima beans, bagels, oil cakes. The smells these delicacies sent out were delicious. I began to fantasize what I would do if I had a million rubles. I would buy all these goodies and make a feast for Shosha. We would munch on chocolate, halvah, tangerines, and take a ride in a sleigh. I would stop going to cheder and have a rabbi tutor me at home.

I was so preoccupied with my reveries I didn't notice that it had started snowing. A dense snow began to fall, dry and grainy as salt. My eyes crusted over. The street gaslights became covered with snow and their shine turned orange, blue, green, violet. This wasn't merely snow but snow mixed with sleet. Chunks of ice fell from the sky and a strong wind began to blow. Maybe the world was coming to an end? It seemed to me that there was thunder and lightning.

I started to run and fell several times. I picked myself up, and to my alarm I saw that I had strayed into some other street. Here, the street lights weren't gas but electric. I saw a trolley that wasn't drawn by horses. The rod extending from

its roof to the wires overhead sprayed bluish
sparks. A fear came over me—I was lost! I stopped
passersby and asked them directions but they ig-
nored me. One person did answer me, but in
Polish, a language I had never learned. I could
barely keep from crying. I wanted to turn back to
where I had come from, but apparently I only
strayed farther away. I passed brightly illuminated
stores and a building with balconies and columns
like some royal palace. Music was playing upstairs
and below, merchants were clearing away their
goods from the stalls. The wind scattered kerchiefs,
handkerchiefs, shirts, and blouses, and they
whirled in the air like imps. That which I had always feared had apparently happened—the evil
spirits had turned their wrath on me.

Now the wind thrust me forward, now it dragged
me back. It blew up the skirt of my coat and tried
to lift me in the air. I knew where the gale sought
to carry me—to Sodom, to beyond the Mountains
of Darkness, to Asmodeus's castle, to Mount Sair
where the ground is copper and the sky is iron. I
wanted to cry out to God, to utter some prayer or
incantation, but my mouth had gone numb and
my nose was stiff as wood. The cold penetrated
through my coat, through both vests. My eyelids
became swollen and I could no longer see in the
white maelstrom.

Suddenly I heard a shrill clanging and shouts.
Someone sprang and, seizing me from behind, half

dragged, half carried me off. Was this a demon, a wraith? A man in a long coat and a black beard turned white from the snow and frost shouted at me in rage. "Where are you running? Where do you creep to? You just missed being run over by the trolley car."

I wanted to thank him but I couldn't utter a word.

The man asked, "Who lets a child out in such a blizzard? You have no parents?"

I still don't know why, but I said, "No, I'm an orphan."

"An orphan, eh? Who do you live with?"

"My grandfather."

"Where does your grandfather live?"

I gave a false address—13 Krochmalna Street.

"What are you doing here if you live at 13 Krochmalna? Got lost, eh?"

"No."

"Where were you going?"

"I wanted to say the mourner's prayer," I replied, astounded by my own lie.

"No synagogues or prayerhouses on Krochmalna? I see that you're lost. Come, I'll take you back."

He took my hand and led me along.

He asked, "What does your grandfather do? How does he make a living?"

"A porter," I said. The words issued from my mouth as if on their own.

"An old man a porter? He's still got the strength to carry? You hungry?"

"No. Yes."

"Wait, I'll get you something."

We walked only a few minutes. I had assumed I had strayed far from Krochmalna, but suddenly I saw it again. I wanted to get away from the man and my lies, but he held me firmly by the hand. He said, "Don't try to run away, boy. Poverty is no disgrace."

He led me into a restaurant. I had passed this restaurant earlier that day. Summer and winter a cloud of steam hovered inside it and it always smelled of fried onions, garlic, meat, soup, beer. At night music was played there. I once heard my mother say that they served food that wasn't strictly kosher and that it was patronized by gangsters, thieves, the rabble. One boor there had bet that he could eat a whole roast goose. He was about to swallow the last bite when he got sick and had to be taken to the hospital. Now I was there myself. The floor was tiled in white and black like a checkerboard. Burly men and fat women sat at tables covered in red. Some ate boiled beef, others drank beer from mugs. Many gaslights were flashing. Waiters in white aprons carried huge trays with dishes above the diners' heads. There were other rooms here; from one came the sounds of singing, an accordion, hands clapping.

The man with me couldn't find a table. He stood

with me in the crush and spoke to everyone and
to no one: "An orphan. Nearly got run over. Hungry, poor thing. Half frozen. Give him something
to eat. It's a good deed!"

He begged in my behalf. Again I tried to slip
away from him, but he held me fast. The walls
here were covered with red tapestries and hung
with mirrors, so that I saw myself many times
over.

A stout woman came up and asked my bene-
factor, "Why are you holding this boy? Has he
done something?"

"Done something? He's done nothing. A poor
orphan and hungry."

"An orphan? He's our rabbi's son. His parents
are living. I saw his mother this very day at the
butcher's."

"Eh? But he told me he was an orphan and that
his grandfather is a porter—"

"A porter? Has he gone mad?"

The man apparently grew so confused that he
let go of my hand. I dashed off. In a moment I was
outside again.

IV

I barely recognized the street. My brother, Joshua, had often spoken of the North Pole and the fact that the nights there lasted six months. Krochmalna Street now appeared to me like the North Pole. Huge mounds of snow had fallen. Whole towers and mountains had formed on the gutter. The pedestrians sank into the snowy depths. Misty trails extended from the street lamps. The sky hung low, reflecting a violet tinge with no moon or stars showing. I tried to run, fearing the man would catch and punish me for my lies. I had committed so many sins! My parents would soon discover that I had deceived the man and posed as an orphan. They would also learn that the assistant teacher had let me walk home alone and that I had gotten lost. The boys at the cheder would have something to mock at and would make up new nicknames for me. The assistant teacher would become my enemy.

Suddenly I recalled a story my brother, Joshua, had told me about a boy who had been sent on a Passover night to open the door for the prophet Elijah and had vanished. Years later he came home a grown man and a professor. He had walked from the town where his parents lived to Warsaw,

and then on to Berlin. Rich people there had helped
him obtain an education. That's what I would have
to do too—run away from home! I would read all
the books about the sun, the moon, the stars. I
would learn how mountains, rivers, oceans, and
the North Pole had formed. My father had one answer for everything—God had created it all. He
wanted me to study only religious books. But the
worldly books obviously had many other explana-
tions.

Joshua often spoke about science. He said that a
cheder education left one ignorant. He spoke of a
telescope through which you could see the mountains and craters of the moon. Since we lived in
Warsaw, I could proceed straight to Berlin. I knew
that a train left for Germany from the Vienna de-
pot. I would simply follow the tracks till I came to
Berlin. But what would my parents do if I didn't
come home? And what about Shosha? I would
miss her terribly. A strange notion came to me:
maybe Shosha would run away with me. In storybooks I often read of boys and girls who left home
together on account of love. True, these were
grownups, but I loved Shosha. I thought of her
during the day and I dreamed about her at night.
We would study together in Berlin, and when I
became a professor, we would marry and come
back to Warsaw. Everyone on Krochmalna Street
would come out to greet us. My mother and Sho-

sha's mother would weep and embrace. By then, everyone would have forgotten the silly things I had done today. The cheder boys who now pushed me around and called me names would come to me to teach them science and philosophy. . .

I had reached the gate of 10 Krochmalna Street, but instead of going home I went to Shosha's. I had to talk to her! In my mind I prayed to God that she would be home alone. Her father worked in a store and her mother often went to shop at the bazaar or to gossip with her sister. This time luck was with me. I knocked and Shosha opened. She seemed frightened by me and she said, "Oh, just look at you! White as a snowman."

It was warm in Shosha's kitchen and I promptly began telling her of my plans. She sat down on a footstool. She was blond, blue-eyed, and wore her hair in braids. She was exceptionally pale. Although she was my age, she was like a child of five. She played with dolls and got poor grades at the Polish school she attended. She couldn't read or figure properly. I now suggested that she accompany me to Berlin. Shosha heard me out calmly, then asked, "What will we eat?"

I was dumfounded. I had completely forgotten that a person had to eat.

After a while I said, "We'll take food from home."

"And where will we sleep?"

I didn't know what to say. The trip to Berlin

would undoubtedly take weeks. In the summer you could sleep outdoors, but in winter it would be too cold. For a moment I wondered at my own stupidity and at Shosha's wisdom. Suddenly the door opened and my mother came in with my sister, Hindele, close behind her.

Hindele exclaimed, "There he is, Mama! What did I tell you?"

Mother stared at me in confusion. "So there you are . . . We've been searching for you two hours. I thought, who knows *what* happened . . ." And all at once she erupted, "Unfaithful child!"

I knew full well the meaning of this expression —a faithless son and a rebellious one. According to the law of the Pentateuch, I should be turned over by my parents to the town elders, who would condemn me to be stoned. An interrogation was forthcoming and I had no excuses ready.

My sister said, "We were waiting for you for the blessing of the Hanukkah candles."

"Where were you all this time? Didn't the assistant teacher bring you?" Mother asked.

"Yes, he brought me."

"When? You've been sitting here two hours?"

"He just came in this second," Shosha said.

"Why were you running around in such a storm? Why did you come here instead of home?"

"He wants us to follow the train tracks . . ." Shosha said, not intending to inform, but simply because she didn't understand the significance of it all.

My sister began to laugh. "He wants to run away with little Shosha! He's carrying on a love affair with her!"

"Don't laugh, Hindele, don't laugh!" Mother said. "The boy is making me sick!"

"Look at him! White as chalk!" my sister observed.

"Come!" Mother said.

She grabbed me by the collar and led me away. I anticipated a severe punishment, but when Father saw me, he only smiled and said, "I'm waiting for you with Hanukkah candles. I have a gift for you too."

"He's got no gifts coming," Mother exclaimed. "He was outside in the cold the whole time. You didn't even ask where I found him!" she reproached Father. "At our neighbor's, at Bashele's!"

"Who is this Bashele?" Father asked.

"Abraham Kaufman's wife."

"What was he doing there?"

"They have a girl, some little fool, and he wants to run away with her."

Father arched his brows. "Oh, so? Well, it's Hanukkah. I don't want to spoil the holiday."

In honor of the holiday Father had donned his velvet housecoat. Our ceiling lamp was lit. The Hanukkah candelabrum stood ready. A red candle —the so-called "sexton"—rested in its holder. Father poured in olive oil and fussed with the wick. He made the benediction and lit a candle with the "sexton." Father's red beard glowed like fire. He took a prayer book with wooden covers from his pocket. It had a carving of the Western Wall on the front cover and one of the Cave of Machpelah on the back.

He said, "This prayer book comes from the Land of Israel."

"From the Land of Israel?"

I took the prayer book with joy and trepidation.
I had never before held an object that stemmed
from this distant and sacred land. It seemed to
me that this prayer book exuded the scent of figs,
dates, carob beans, cloves, cedar. All the stories
from the Scriptures suddenly came to mind: of
Sodom, of the Dead Sea, of Rachel's Tomb, of
Joseph's dreams, of the ladder the angels climbed
up to and down from heaven, as well as of King
David, King Solomon, the Queen of Sheba.

My sister, Hindele, said, "Why does he get a
gift?" And she added, "The worst dog gets the best
bone."

"You'll see that the boy will cause us shame and
disgrace!" Mother complained. "I don't believe that
the assistant teacher brought him here at all. He
always brings him into the house."

"Well, it's a holiday, a holiday!" Father said half
to us, half to himself.

"You'll spoil him so, he'll become completely
wild," Mother warned.

"With the Almighty's help, he'll grow up a decent
man," Father said. He turned to me. "Pray from
this book. Everything that comes from the Land
of Israel is holy. This Wall is a remnant of the
Holy Temple, which the evildoers demolished. The
Divine Presence reigns there forever. Jews sinned;
that's why the Temple was destroyed. But the Almighty is all-merciful. He is our Father and we are

His children. God willing, the Messiah will come and we'll all go back to our homeland. A fiery Temple will descend upon Jerusalem. The dead will be resurrected. Our grandfathers, grandmothers, great-grandfathers, and all the generations will live again. The light of the sun will be seven times brighter than now. The saints will sit with crowns upon their heads and study the secrets of the Torah."

"Mama, the potato pancakes are getting cold," Hindele said.

"Oh yes!"

And my mother and sister went back to the kitchen.

"Where did you go?" Father asked. "It's freezing outside. You might have caught cold, God forbid. You'd be better off glancing into a holy book."

"Papa, I'd like to study science," I said, astounded at my own words.

"Science? What kind of science"

"Why summer is warm and winter is cold. How high is the moon and what happens up on the stars. How deep is the earth and how tall is the sky. Everything . . . everything . . ."

"All knowledge is contained in the Torah," Father replied. "Every letter of the Torah conceals countless secrets and infinite depth. Those who study the cabala acquire more truth than all the philosophers."

"Papa, teach me the cabala."

"Cabala isn't for boys. You may not study the cabala until you're thirty."

"I want it now!"

"Wait. You're still a child. What do you do there at the neighbors'? Who is that little girl? Since she's a fool, what do you need with her?"

"She is *not* a fool."

"Eh? Then what is she?"

"She is good. The boys at cheder call me names, but she is nice to me. When we grow up, I want to marry her," I said, baffled by my own words. It was as if a dybbuk had spoken out of me and I was overcome with fear.

Father smiled, but he promptly grew earnest. "Everything comes from heaven. It's said that forty days before a person is born, an angel in heaven calls out: 'This one's daughter will marry that one's son.' What's this girl's name?"

"Shosha."

"Shosha? I had an Aunt Shosha. She was my aunt and your great-aunt."

"Where does she live?"

"Aunt Shosha? In heaven, in paradise. She was a saint. She would go to the Belz Rabbi and he would place her in a seat of honor. In her old age she went to the Land of Israel and there she died. Oh, I have another gift for you, a dreidel."

The door opened and Mother and Hindele brought in the potato pancakes. During the brief time Mother had been in the kitchen her face had relaxed. My sister was smiling. I showed Mother the shining, new dreidel and she gave me a sharp glance.

"You got lost, eh?"

I wanted to deny it, but I could not speak from too much happiness. Besides, she knew everything, just like a prophetess. She often read my mind. Her big gray eyes seemed to say, "I know all your antics but I love you anyhow."

The Fools of Chelm
and the Stupid Carp

In Chelm, a city of fools, every housewife bought fish for the Sabbath. The rich bought large fish, the poor small ones. They were bought on Thursday, cut up, chopped, and made into gefilte fish on Friday, and eaten on the Sabbath.

One Thursday morning the door opened at the house of the community leader of Chelm, Gronam Ox, and Zeinvel Ninny entered, carrying a trough full of water. Inside was a large, live carp.

"What is this?" Gronam asked.

"A gift to you from the wise men of Chelm," Zeinvel said. "This is the largest carp ever caught in the Lake of Chelm, and we all decided to give it to you as a token of appreciation for your great wisdom."

"Thank you very much," Gronam Ox replied. "My wife, Yente Pesha, will be delighted. She and I both love carp. I read in a book that eating the brains of a carp increases wisdom, and even though we in Chelm are immensely clever, a little improvement never hurts. But let me have a close look at him. I was told that a carp's tail shows the size of his brain."

Gronam Ox was known to be nearsighted, and when he bent down to the trough to better observe the carp's tail, the carp did something that proved he was not as wise as Gronam thought. He lifted his tail and smacked Gronam across the face.

Gronam Ox was flabbergasted. "Something like this never happened to me before," he exclaimed. "I cannot believe this carp was caught in the Chelm lake. A Chelm carp would know better."

"He's the meanest fish I ever saw in my life," agreed Zeinvel Ninny.

Even though Chelm is a big city, news traveled quickly there. In no time at all the other wise men of Chelm arrived at the house of their leader, Gronam Ox. Treitel Fool came, and Sender Donkey, Shmendrick Numskull, and Dopey Lekisch. Gronam Ox was saying, "I'm not going to eat this fish on the Sabbath. This carp is a fool, and malicious to boot. If I eat him, I could become foolish instead of cleverer."

"Then what shall I do with him?" asked Zeinvel Ninny.

Gronam Ox put a finger to his head as a sign that he was thinking hard. After a while he cried out, "No man or animal in Chelm should slap Gronam Ox. This fish should be punished."

"What kind of punishment shall we give him?" asked Treitel Fool. "All fish are killed anyhow, and one cannot kill a fish twice."

"He shouldn't be killed like other fish," Sender Donkey said. "He should die in a different way to show that no one can smack our beloved sage, Gronam Ox, and get away with it."

"What kind of death?" wondered Shmendrick Numskull. "Shall we perhaps just imprison him?"

"There is no prison in Chelm for fish," said Zeinvel Ninny. "And to build such a prison would take too long."

"Maybe he should be hanged," suggested Dopey Lekisch.

"How do you hang a carp?" Sender Donkey wanted to know. "A creature can be hanged only by its neck, but since a carp has no neck, how will you hang him?"

"My advice is that he should be thrown to the dogs alive," said Treitel Fool.

"It's no good," Gronam Ox answered. "Our

Chelm dogs are both smart and modest, but if
they eat this carp, they may become as stupid
and mean as he is."

"So what should we do?" all the wise men asked.

"This case needs lengthy consideration," Gronam Ox decided. "Let's leave the carp in the
trough and ponder the matter as long as is neces-
sary. Being the wisest man in Chelm, I cannot
afford to pass a sentence that will not be admired
by all the Chelmites."

"If the carp stays in the trough a long time,
he may die," Zeinvel Ninny, a former fish dealer,
explained. "To keep him alive we must put him
into a large tub, and the water has to be changed
often. He must also be fed properly."

"You are right, Zeinvel," Gronam Ox told him.
"Go and find the largest tub in Chelm and see to
it that the carp is kept alive and healthy until the
day of judgment. When I reach a decision, you
will hear about it."

Of course Gronam's words were the law in
Chelm. The five wise men went and found a large
tub, filled it with fresh water, and put the criminal
carp in it, together with some crumbs of bread,
challah, and other tidbits a carp might like to eat.
Shlemiel, Gronam's bodyguard, was stationed at
the tub to make sure that no greedy Chelmite wife
would use the imprisoned carp for gefilte fish.

It just so happened that Gronam Ox had many
other decisions to make, and he kept postponing

the sentence. The carp seemed not to be impatient. He ate, swam in the tub, became even fatter than he had been, not realizing that a severe sentence hung over his head. Shlemiel changed the water frequently, because he was told that if the carp died, this would be an act of contempt for Gronam Ox and for the Chelm Court of Justice. Yukel the water carrier made a few extra pennies every day by bringing water for the carp. Some of the Chelmites who were in opposition to Gronam Ox spread the gossip that Gronam just couldn't find the right type of punishment for the carp and that he was waiting for the carp to die a natural death. But, as always, a great disappointment awaited them. One morning about half a year later, the sentence became known, and when it was known, Chelm was stunned. The carp had to be drowned.

Gronam Ox had thought up many clever sentences before, but never one as brilliant as this one. Even his enemies were amazed at this shrewd verdict. Drowning is just the kind of death suited to a spiteful carp with a large tail and a small brain.

That day the entire Chelm community gathered at the lake to see the sentence executed. The carp, which had become almost twice as big as he had been before, was brought to the lake in the wagon that carried the worst criminals to their death. The drummers drummed. Trumpets blared. The Chelmite executioner raised the heavy carp and threw it into the lake with a mighty splash.

A great cry rose from the Chelmites. "Down with the treacherous carp! Long live Gronam Ox! Hurrah!"

Gronam was lifted by his admirers and carried home with songs of praise. Some Chelmite girls showered him with flowers. Even Yente Pesha, his wife, who was often critical of Gronam and dared to call him fool, seemed impressed by Gronam's high intelligence.

In Chelm, as everywhere else, there were envious people who found fault with everyone, and they began to say that there was no proof whatsoever that the carp really drowned. Why should a carp drown in lake water? they asked. While hundreds of innocent fish were killed every Friday, they said, that stupid carp lived in comfort for months on the taxpayers' money and then was returned sound and healthy to the lake, where he is laughing at Chelm justice.

But only a few listened to these malicious words. They pointed out that months passed and the carp was never caught again, a sure sign that he was dead. It is true that the carp just might have decided to be careful and to avoid the fisherman's net. But how can a foolish carp who slaps Gronam Ox have such wisdom?

Just the same, to be on the safe side, the wise men of Chelm published a decree that if the nasty carp had refused to be drowned and was caught again, a special jail should be built for him, a pool where he would be kept prisoner for the rest of his life.

The decree was printed in capital letters in the official gazette of Chelm and signed by Gronam Ox and his five sages—Treitel Fool, Sender Donkey, Shmendrick Numskull, Zeinvel Ninny, and Dopey Lekisch.

Lemel and Tzipa

This story was told me by my mother, and I'm retelling it here word for word, as closely as possible.

Once there was a well-to-do countryman named Tobias, and he and his wife, Leah, had a daughter, Tzipa, who was a fool the likes of which you couldn't find in the entire region. When Tzipa grew up, marriage brokers began to propose matches for her, but as soon as a prospective groom came to look her over and she began to spout her nonsense, he would flee from her. It appeared that Tzipa would be left an old maid.

The husband and wife went to ask advice of a rabbi, who told them, "Marriages are made in heaven. Since Tzipa is a fool, heaven will surely provide a foolish groom for her. Just ask around about a youth who's a bigger fool than your daughter, and when the two fools marry, they'll be happy together."

The parents were pleased by this advice. They went to a matchmaker and told him to find the biggest fool in the Lublin province for their daughter. They promised the matchmaker double the fee usually paid for arranging a match. The matchmaker knew that no city contained so many fools as Chelm, so that was where he headed.

He came to a house and saw a youth sitting in front of it and crying. The matchmaker asked, "Young fellow, why are you crying?"

And the youth said, "My mother baked a whole dish of blintzes for Shevuoth. When she went out to buy sour cream for the blintzes, she warned me, 'Lemel, don't eat the blintzes until Shevuoth.' I promised her that I wouldn't, but the moment she left the house I got a great urge for a blintz and I ate one, and after the first I got the urge for another, and a third, and a fourth, and before you know it, I finished the whole dish of blintzes. I was so busy eating blintzes I didn't see the cat watching me. Now I'm very much afraid that when

Mother comes back the cat will tell her what I've done and Mother will pinch me and call me what she calls me anyhow—fool, oaf, dummy, ninny, simp, clod, donkey."

"This Lemel is made for Tzipa," the matchmaker thought.

Aloud he said, "I know how to speak the cat language. I'll tell the cat to say nothing, and when I give a cat an order he listens, for I am the King of the Cats."

Hearing these words, Lemel commenced to dance with joy. The matchmaker began to utter fabricated words to the cat—whatever came to his lips: "Petche-metche-ketche-letche."

Then he asked, "Lemel, do you want a bride?"

"Certainly!"

"I have just the bride for you—no one like her in the whole world. Tzipa is her name."

"Does she have red cheeks?" Lemel asked. "I like a girl with red cheeks and long braids."

"She has everything you want."

Lemel began to dance anew and clap his hands. At that moment his mother came in with the pot of sour cream. When she saw her son dancing, she asked, "Lemel, what's the big celebration about?"

And Lemel replied, "I ate up all the blintzes and I was afraid the cat would tell, but this man ordered the cat not to talk."

"Dummox! Dolt!" the mother screamed. "What

will I do with you? What girl would want to marry such a dunderhead?"

"Mama, I have a bride already!" Lemel exclaimed. "Her name is Tzipa and she has long cheeks and red braids."

A few days later Lemel and Tzipa drew up their articles of engagement. They could not write their names and Lemel signed with three dots and Tzipa with three dashes. Lemel got a dowry of two hundred gulden. Since Lemel didn't understand about money and didn't know the difference between one banknote and another, Tzipa's father wrapped the five-gulden notes in white paper and the ten-gulden notes in blue paper. Lemel also got a silver watch, but since he couldn't read figures, when he wanted to know the time he stopped a person in the street and asked, "What time is it?" At the same time he added, "I can't see because I've lost my glasses." This was what his mother had told him to use as an excuse.

When the day of the wedding came, Tzipa began to weep bitterly.

Her mother asked, "Tzipa, why are you crying?"

And Tzipa replied, "I'm ashamed to marry a stranger."

The mother said, "I married a stranger too. After the wedding, the husband and wife become close and are no longer strangers."

But Tzipa countered, "You, Mama, married Papa, but I have to marry a complete stranger."

The mother said, "Tzipa, you're a big fool but your groom is a fool too and together you'll be, God willing, two happy fools."

After lengthy discussions, Tzipa allowed herself to be escorted to the wedding canopy.

Some time after the wedding, Tzipa's father said to his son-in-law, "Lemel, your father is a merchant, I'm a merchant, and I want you to be a merchant too. I've given you a dowry. Use it to go into business."

"What's a merchant?" Lemel asked, and his father-in-law said, "A merchant is someone who buys cheap and sells dear. That's how he makes a profit. Take the dowry, go to Lublin, and if you spot a bargain there, buy it as cheaply as possible, then come back here and sell it at a high price."

Lemel did as his father-in-law ordered. Tzipa gave him a chicken wrapped in cabbage leaves for the road. In the wagon, Lemel got hungry and wanted to eat the chicken, but it was raw. Tzipa's mother had told her to give her husband a chicken, but since she didn't say anything about cooking it, Tzipa had given Lemel a raw chicken.

Lemel stopped at an inn. He was very hungry. They asked him what he wanted to eat and he said, "Give me everything you have and I'll eat until I'm full."

Said and done. First they gave him a glass of wine, then another; than an appetizer of tripe with calf's foot. Lemel ate this with lots of bread

and horseradish. Then they served him a bowl of
noodle soup. After Lemel had finished one bowl
of soup, he asked for another. Then they served
Lemel a huge portion of meat with groats, cabbage, potatoes, and carrots. Lemel finished everything and was still hungry. Then they served him
a compote of prunes, apples, pears, and raisins.
Lemel gulped it all down and yet his hunger was
still not sated. Finally, they served him tea with
sponge cake and honey cake. Lemel drank the
tea and ate the cake, but somehow the hunger still
gnawed at him. The innkeeper said, "I hope that
by now you are full."

But Lemel replied, "No, I'm still hungry."

The innkeeper took a cookie out of the cabinet
and said, "Try this."

Lemel ate the cookie and immediately felt sated.
He said, "Now I'm full. Had I known that you can
get full from a cookie, I needn't have ordered all
those other dishes."

The innkeeper promptly saw that he was dealing with a dolt. He himself was a swindler and he said, "Now it's too late. But if you ever come here again, I'll give you such a cookie right off the bat and you won't have to order the other dishes. Now, be so good as to pay for the meal."

Lemel took from his purse the banknotes rolled in white paper and those rolled in blue paper and he said, "One paper contains the five-gulden bills and the other the ten-gulden bills, but I don't remember which is which."

The innkeeper unrolled the two stacks, and as befits a swindler, he told Lemel that a ten-gulden was a five-gulden bill. He also swindled Lemel with the change.

In Lublin Lemel went from store to store seeking bargains, but somehow there were no bargains to be found. Lying in bed at night, Lemel began to think about the miraculous cookie which made you instantly full. "If I knew how to bake such cookies I'd be rich," Lemel said to himself. "There isn't enough food in Chelm, the people are hungry, and everyone would welcome such cookies."

He himself had felt sated for nearly twenty hours after eating this cookie.

The next day Lemel headed home and he stopped at the same inn. He ordered the miraculous cookie, but the innkeeper said, "I just now served the last of them to a guest. But I can sell you the recipe. Believe me, when you bake these cookies in Chelm you'll sell them for a big profit and you'll become as rich as Rothschild."

"What does this recipe cost?"

The innkeeper named a high price, but Lemel decided that by baking such cookies he could get back all the money he would pay, with a huge profit besides. So he bought the recipe. Having already seen that Lemel couldn't read, write, or even determine the value of a coin, the innkeeper composed the following recipe:

> Take three quarts of duck's milk, five pounds of flour ground from iron, two pounds of cheese made from snow, one pound of fat from a flintstone, a half pound of feathers from a red crow, and a quarter pound of juice squeezed from copper. Throw it all in a pot made of wax and let it cook three days and three nights over the fire of a potato tree. After three days, knead a dough out of the mixture, cut out the cookies with a knife made of butter, and bake them in an oven made of ice till they turn red, brown, and yellow. Then dig a pit, throw in the whole mess, and put up a board with a sign over it reading: WHEN YOU SEND A FOOL TO MARKET, THE MERCHANTS REJOICE.

After Lemel finished paying for the meal and the recipe, he barely had enough left for the fare home.

But he was pleased with the bargain he had made.

When he came home and told Tzipa about the miraculous cookie, she began to clap her hands and dance. But the joy didn't last long. When Lemel's father-in-law came home and read the recipe, he became furious and screamed, "Lemel, you've been swindled!"

Tzipa promptly began to cry. Tzipa's mother cried along with her.

After a while, Lemel said, "All my troubles stem from the fact that I can't read. I must learn to read, and the quicker the better."

"Yes, my son," Tzipa's father said. "A merchant must be able to read and write."

Since there were no teachers in the village, Lemel resolved to go to Lublin to learn to read. Again, the father-in-law gave him money for the fare and to pay for the lessons. In Lublin, Lemel went to Lewartow Street to seek out a teacher. He walked past a store displaying eyeglasses in the window. He looked inside and saw a customer put on a pair of glasses and glance into a book while the proprietor asked, "Now can you read?"

"Yes, now I can read well," the customer said.

Lemel thought to himself, "Since putting on glasses enables you to read, what do I need with a teacher?"

Lemel had no urge to study. He yearned to go home to Tzipa.

He went into the store and said to the proprietor,

"Give me a pair of glasses so that I can read."

The proprietor asked what strength glasses he had worn before and Lemel said, "I don't know anything about it. Let me test them."

The proprietor handed him a pair of glasses and opened a book before him.

Lemel looked into the book and said, "I can't read."

"I'll give you stronger glasses," the proprietor said.

Lemel tested the second pair and said, "I still can't read."

The proprietor offered him many different glasses to try but Lemel kept giving the same answer—he still couldn't read.

After a while, the proprietor said, "Forgive me, but maybe you can't read at all?"

"If I could read, I wouldn't have come to you in the first place," Lemel said.

"In that case, you must first go to a teacher and learn to read. You can't learn to read from putting on a pair of glasses," the storekeeper said.

Lemel grew depressed by the answer. He had been prepared to put on the glasses and go back home. After a while Lemel decided that he couldn't go on without Tzipa. He missed her terribly. He went to seek out a teacher not so much to learn how to read as to have the teacher write a letter home for him. He soon found one. When Lemel asked how long it would take for him to learn to read, the teacher said, "It could take a year, but not less than a half year."

Lemel grew very sad. He said to the teacher, "Could you write a letter for me? I want to send a letter to my Tzipa."

"Yes, I could write a letter for you. Tell me what to write."

Lemel began to dictate:

Dear Tzipa,

I'm already in Lublin. I thought that if you put on glasses you could read, but the proprietor of the store said that glasses don't help. The teacher says it would take a half year or a whole year to teach me to read and that I would have to stay here in Lublin the whole time. Dear Tzipele, I love you so much that when I'm away from you one day I must die of longing. If I am without you for a half year, I'll have to die maybe a hundred times or even more. Therefore, I've decided to come home, if my father-in-law, your father, will agree. I hope to find some kind of work for which you don't have to read or write.

Longingly,
Your Lemel

*   *   *

When Tzipa received this letter and her father
read it to her, she burst into tears and dictated a
letter to Lemel which read as follows:

Dear Lemel,

When you don't see me for a day you must
die, but when I don't see you for a minute, I
go crazy. Yes, my dear Lemel, come back. I
don't need a writer but a good husband and,
later, a houseful of children—six boys and
six girls. Father will find some kind of work
for you. Don't wait but come straight home,
because if you come back dead and find me
crazy, it wouldn't be so good for either of us.

Your devoted Tzipa

When the teacher read Tzipa's letter to Lemel he
burst out crying. That very same day he started
for home. Before getting into the wagon in Lublin,
he went to the market to buy a present for Tzipa.
He went into a mirror store with the intention of
buying her a mirror. At the same time he told the
storekeeper everything that had happened to him
—how he had been swindled with the cookie and
how he had been unable to learn to read with the
glasses.

The storekeeper was a prankster and dishonest
as well. He said: "Such people as you, Lemel, and

your wife, Tzipa, should be many. I have a potion which when you drink it will make you become double, triple, quadruple. How would you like there to be ten Lemels and ten Tzipas who would all love each other? One Lemel and one Tzipa could stay home all day, another set could go to market to buy goods, a third set could take a walk, a fourth set could eat blintzes with sour cream, and the fifth set could go to Lublin and learn to read and write."

"How is this possible?" Lemel asked.

"Drink the potion and you'll see for yourself."

The storekeeper gave Lemel a glass of plain water and told him to drink merely one drop of it. Then he led Lemel into a room where two mirrors hung facing each other, one of which was tilted slightly to the side. When Lemel came into the room he saw not one Lemel in the mirror but a whole row of Lemels. He walked over to the other mirror and there were many Lemels there too.

The storekeeper stood by the door and said, "Well, did I deceive you?"

"Oh, I can't believe my own eyes!" Lemel exclaimed. "How much is this potion?"

"It's very expensive," the storekeeper said, "but for you, I'll make it cheap. Give me all the money you have except for your fare home. You've snagged a terrific bargain."

Lemel paid on the spot and the storekeeper gave him a big bottle filled with water. He told him,

"You and your Tzipa need drink only one drop a day. This bottle will last you for years. If it gets used up, you can always come back to Lublin and I'll refill it for you for free. Wait, I'll give you a written guarantee."

The storekeeper took out a sheet of paper and wrote on it: "God loves fools. That's why He made so many of them."

When Lemel came home and his father-in-law saw the bottle of water and read the note, he realized that Lemel had been swindled again.

But when Lemel saw Tzipa his joy was so intense he forgot all his troubles. He kissed and hugged her and cried, "I don't need many Tzipas. One Tzipa is enough for me, even if I should live to be a thousand!"

"And I don't need many Lemels. One Lemel is enough for me, even if I should live to be a million!" Tzipa exclaimed.

Yes, Lemel and Tzipa were both fools, but they possessed more love than all the sages. After a while, Lemel bought a horse and wagon and became a coachman. For this he didn't have to know how to read or write. He drove passengers to and from Chelm and everyone liked him for his punctuality, his friendliness, and for the love he showed his horse. Tzipa began to have children and bore Lemel six boys and six girls. The boys took after Tzipa and the girls after Lemel, but they were all good-natured fools and they all found mates in Chelm. Lemel and Tzipa lived happily to a ripe old age, long enough to enjoy a whole tribe of grandchildren, great-grandchildren, and great-great-grandchildren.

The Cat Who Thought She Was a Dog and the Dog Who Thought He Was a Cat

Once there was a poor peasant, Jan Skiba by name. He lived with his wife and three daughters in a one-room hut with a straw roof, far from the village. The house had a bed, a bench bed, and a stove, but no mirror. A mirror was a luxury for a poor peasant. And why would a peasant need a mirror? Peasants aren't curious about their appearance.

But this peasant did have a dog and a cat in his hut. The dog was named Burek and the cat Kot.

They had both been born within the same week. As little food as the peasant had for himself and his family, he still wouldn't let his dog and cat go hungry. Since the dog had never seen another dog and the cat had never seen another cat and they saw only each other, the dog thought he was a cat and the cat thought she was a dog. True, they were far from being alike by nature. The dog barked and the cat meowed. The dog chased rabbits and the cat lurked after mice. But must all creatures be exactly like their own kind? The peasant's children weren't exactly alike either. Burek and Kot lived on good terms, often ate from the same dish, and tried to mimic each other. When Burek barked, Kot tried to bark along, and when Kot meowed, Burek tried to meow too. Kot occasionally chased rabbits and Burek made an effort to catch a mouse.

The peddlers who bought groats, chickens, eggs, honey, calves, and whatever was available from the peasants in the village never came to Jan Skiba's poor hut. They knew that Jan was so poor he had nothing to sell. But one day a peddler happened to stray there. When he came inside and began to lay out his wares, Jan Skiba's wife and daughters were bedazzled by all the pretty doodads. From his sack the peddler drew yellow beads, false pearls, tin earrings, rings, brooches, colored kerchiefs, garters, and other such trinkets. But what enthralled the women of the house most was a mirror set in a wooden frame. They asked the

peddler its price and he said a half gulden, which
was a lot of money for poor peasants. After a while,
Jan Skiba's wife, Marianna, made a proposition to
the peddler. She would pay him five groshen a
month for the mirror. The peddler hesitated a
moment. The mirror took up too much space in
his sack and there was always the danger it might
break. He, therefore, decided to go along, took the
first payment of five groshen from Marianna, and
left the mirror with the family. He visited the region often and he knew the Skibas to be honest
people. He would gradually get his money back and
a profit besides.

The mirror created a commotion in the hut.
Until then Marianna and the children had seldom
seen themselves. Before they had the mirror, they
had only seen their reflections in the barrel of water that stood by the door. Now they could see
themselves clearly and they began to find defects
in their faces, defects they had never noticed before. Marianna was pretty but she had a tooth
missing in front and she felt that this made her
ugly. One daughter discovered that her nose was
too snub and too broad; a second that her chin
was too narrow and too long; a third that her face
was sprinkled with freckles. Jan Skiba too caught
a glimpse of himself in the mirror and grew dis-
pleased by his thick lips and his teeth, which pro-
truded like a buck's. That day, the women of the
house became so absorbed in the mirror they didn't

cook supper, didn't make up the bed, and neglected all the other household tasks. Marianna had heard of a dentist in the big city who could replace a missing tooth, but such things were expensive. The girls tried to console each other that they were pretty enough and that they would find suitors, but they no longer felt as jolly as before. They had been afflicted with the vanity of city girls. The one with the broad nose kept trying to pinch it together with her fingers to make it narrower; the one with the too-long chin pushed it up with her fist to make it shorter; the one with the freckles wondered if there was a salve in the city that could remove freckles. But where would the money come from for the fare to the city? And what about the money to buy this salve? For the first time the Skiba family deeply felt its poverty and envied the rich.

But the human members of the household were not the only ones affected. The dog and the cat also grew disturbed by the mirror. The hut was low and the mirror had been hung just above a bench. The first time the cat sprang up on the bench and saw her image in the mirror, she became terribly perplexed. She had never before seen such a creature. Kot's whiskers bristled, she began to meow at her reflection and raised a paw to it, but the other creature meowed back and raised her paw too. Soon the dog jumped up on the bench, and when he saw the other dog he became wild

with rage and shock. He barked at the other dog
and showed him his teeth, but the other barked
back and bared his fangs too. So great was the
distress of Burek and Kot that for the first time
in their lives they turned on each other. Burek took
a bite out of Kot's throat and Kot hissed and spat
at him and clawed his muzzle. They both started
to bleed and the sight of blood aroused them so
that they nearly killed or crippled each other. The
members of the household barely managed to sep-
arate them. Because a dog is stronger than a cat,
Burek had to be tied outside, and he howled all
day and all night. In their anguish, both the dog
and the cat stopped eating.

When Jan Skiba saw the disruption the mirror had created in his household, he decided a mirror wasn't what his family needed. "Why look at yourself," he said, "when you can see and admire the sky, the sun, the moon, the stars, and the earth, with all its forests, meadows, rivers, and plants?" He took the mirror down from the wall and put it away in the woodshed. When the peddler came for his monthly installment, Jan Skiba gave him back the mirror and in its stead, bought kerchiefs and slippers for the women. After the mirror disappeared, Burek and Kot returned to normal. Again Burek thought he was a cat and Kot was sure she was a dog. Despite all the defects the girls had found in themselves, they made good marriages. The village priest heard what had happened at Jan Skiba's house and he said, "A glass mirror shows only the skin of the body. The real image of a person is in his willingness to help himself and his family and, as far as possible, all those he comes in contact with. This kind of mirror reveals the very soul of the person."

Growing Up

I

The whole night I kept dreaming. What I dreamed, I couldn't recall later, but they must have been fantastic dreams full of youthful valor, for I awoke feeling strong and cheerful. Everything was pleasurable—washing with the cold water at the sink; putting on the gabardine and fringed garment; even praying from the new prayer book with the large type. At the age of eleven I already understood the meaning of the Hebrew words—"How goodly are thy tents, Jacob, thy tabernacles, O

Israel. As for me, in the abundance of thy loving kindness will I come into thy house."

In my fantasy I envisioned the city of Jerusalem and the Holy Temple. The Messiah had come and the Resurrection had taken place. I donned the robes of a priest about to offer a sacrifice. I saw the altar, the table with the shewbread, the Ark, the cherubim—all in gold. And beyond stretched Mount Zion and the mighty city of Jerusalem, with its walls, gates, and flat-roofed houses. King David again occupied his royal throne, and his son Solomon learned the language of lions, tigers, eagles, and the woodcock. The light of the sun was seven times brighter than ever. A day was as long as a year. Everything that had ever been existed once again. All my ancestors, going back to Adam and Eve, had risen from their graves. There was no more death, injustice, only happiness and divine revelation.

At the same time I knew full well that all this was just in my head. Actually, I was in Warsaw, my father was a poor neighborhood rabbi, the land of Israel belonged to the Turks, the Temple lay in ruins. David, Solomon, Bathsheba, and the Queen of Sheba were all dead. My friend was not a prince of the Kingdom of Israel but Black Feivel, whose father was a porter in Janash's bazaar and whose mother sold crockery in the marketplace. Until just a few weeks ago I had attended cheder on Twarda Street, but I had stopped going because my father couldn't afford the two rubles a month tuition.

I rushed through my prayers and breakfast. For weeks Feivel and I had been formulating a secret, outlandish plan. This was the day I was to become a writer and Feivel a printer. I would soon publish my first book—all of sixteen pages long. Its price would be two kopecks. Feivel and I had figured it all out with precision. There were at least fifty thousand boys and girls in Warsaw who liked to read storybooks. If every boy and girl bought my book, we would take in a hundred thousand kopecks, or a thousand rubles. With this sum we could buy our own printing shop and publish additional books. We would accumulate so much money that we would be able to take a ship to the Land of Israel.

This trip was vital not only for us but for all the Jews in the world. Someone had told me that in Jerusalem there was a cave where cabalists sat seeking a hidden name of God that would bring the Messiah. This name had come in a dream to me, Isaac, son of Pinhos Menahem. An angel with six wings had shown himself to me and uttered the name, which consisted of twenty-four letters. The angel had warned me not to utter this name in any other city except Jerusalem. If my lips let it slip in Warsaw, the sky would turn red and the whole world would be consumed by fire.

For a while I had kept this secret to myself, but

one day I blurted it out to Feivel. It happened while we were walking on Senators Street to see the courtyard of the Warsaw firemen, its huge fire bell and the tower with the circular balcony where a fireman walked round and round on the lookout for fires. This tower was so tall that the fireman, a fully grown man, looked like a toy from below. When the sunlight struck his brass helmet, it glowed as if it were on fire.

The situation was this—sometime before, Black Feivel had found a silver forty-kopeck piece and had confided to me his delight over this windfall. Feivel was a year older than I, but he listened to me as if I were his senior. He loved to hear my stories. Not a day went by that I didn't make up some tale about kings, demons, savages, giants, dwarfs, treasures, villians. I had boasted to him that I was versed in the cabala. Feivel's faith in me was like that of a Hasid in his rabbi. I had told him that I was possessed by the spirit of Joseph della Rinah, a saint who centuries before had captured Satan and put him in chains. Had Satan remained so confined, Rabbi Joseph could have brought the Messiah at that time, but he had taken pity on Satan, who had cried and bemoaned his fate and pleaded with Rabbi Joseph for something to eat or drink, or at least for a pinch of snuff. When Rabbi Joseph gave him the snuff, Satan broke into hellish laughter and two sparks shot from his nostrils. Right after that, the chains crumpled from his

body and he flew away along with ten thousand
demons to Mount Sair near Sodom, where the Dark
Powers hold sway.

I told Feivel that Rabbi Joseph's soul had entered my body and that I was destined to carry out
what he had commenced.

II

The practical plan was this: Black Feivel had
found an incredible bargain for a gulden—a case
of rubber type, a pad for ink, and a kind of com-
posing stick into which to set the rubber type to
form words. There was even a brush with which
to pull proofs. Feivel would serve as the typesetter
and printer, and I would be the author. Until we
launched ourselves on a grander scale, I would get
the paper from Father's notebooks, into which he
wrote his interpretations of the Talmud. All we
lacked was a place to do our work. But after an intense search, Feivel found what he was after—a
Hasidic studyhouse that stood empty all day. It was
used only in the mornings and evenings for services. I knew full well that what we were doing was
fraught with danger. The beadle or someone else
was liable to drop in and catch us at it. Nor would

it be easy to go around selling these books, but
Feivel and I had grown so enthused about the writing, the publishing, and the big profits that we had
become bedazzled by it all. Feivel had already set
my name as well as the title page of my first book,
Into the Wild Forest.

This was to be the story of a boy, Haiml, whose
mother had died and whose father had been re-
married to a wicked woman. The stepmother
caused the boy so much grief that he ran away
from home and went to live in the woods. He found
a hollow in a big tree, a thousand-year-old oak, and
he settled there. He lived on berries, mushrooms,
and the other foodstuffs found in a forest. Everything would have been fine, but one night Haiml
heard the soft moaning of a girl. It soon turned out
that this hollow was the entrance to an underground cave where a monster by the name of Mordush lived. This monster had kidnapped a girl,
Rebecca, the daughter of a wealthy man, and was
trying to force her to become his wife. But Rebecca
was engaged already to a young man named Ben
Zion, a rabbi's son, and she didn't want to trade
him for an old villain who had only one eye in the
middle of his forehead and who ate human flesh.
Mordush even tried to make a cannibal out of her,
but Rebecca swore that she would sooner starve
to death than eat the flesh of a human being who
had just recently lived, hoped, and loved . . .

I was supposed to plan out this story to its end

this very night. Ben Zion had to rescue Rebecca and take revenge upon Mordush, and Haiml also had to receive some sort of reward for uncovering the crime. But somehow my creative juices dried up at this point and I couldn't continue the thread of the story. In the process of writing I had grown so attached to Rebecca that I desired her for myself. Actually, in this story, Haiml (who was really myself) was only eleven years old and Rebecca was sixteen, and this would hardly have been a suitable match, but what prevented me from adding a few years to Haiml? I had to find some way to dispose of Ben Zion. Should he die of longing? Should he become a hermit? Should he forget Rebecca and marry the daughter of some magnate? I had just launched my writing career and already I had fallen into a literary dilemma.

When I went down later to meet Feivel, I envied the boys playing tag, hide-and-seek, cops-and-robbers, and nuts, who didn't have to worry about plots and stories. I had prematurely assumed the duties of a writer and publisher, a printer already awaited my efforts, and I knew somehow that I would bear this burden as long as I lived . . .

III

The plan to publish a book had fallen through. First of all, Feivel had lost several of the rubber characters. Second, I couldn't find the right paper in my father's desk drawer. Third, each time we went to the study-house we encountered several youths swaying over open volumes. Fourth, I hadn't found a way of getting rid of Ben Zion and the whole story would have to be rewritten. Feivel said it couldn't be otherwise but that Satan had gotten wind of our plan and had arranged it that I couldn't go to Jerusalem and bring the Messiah.

We roved the streets of Warsaw with the impetus of those against whom all the evils have combined to conspire. My velvet cap was pushed back onto my nape, my red earlocks were drenched with sweat, the wide fringed garment peeped out from my unbuttoned gabardine. Despite my youth, my parents dressed me in rabbinical fashion. They wanted me to become a rabbi. Each time I passed a mirror I grew frightened at my own appearance. My hair was as red as fire, my face and neck an unusual white. A frenzied eagerness shone from my blue eyes. I was fully aware that I was too

young to probe into the cabala. I had often heard
my father say that those who tried to study the
cabala before thirty went crazy or slid into heresy.
At times it seemed to me that I *was* actually crazy.
Wild notions flashed through my brain, fantasies
that I could not bridle. Now I was an emperor and
now a sorcerer; now I donned a cap that rendered
me invisible, and now I flew to the moon and
brought back treasures of gold and diamonds and
a potion that rendered me wiser than King Solomon and stronger than Samson. Instead of bringing the Messiah, in my imagination I became the
Messiah himself. I blew the ram's horn so that its
blast resounded around the world. I mounted a
cloud and flew to Jerusalem, followed by hordes of
angels ready to do my bidding.

Feivel was taller than I. His earlocks were so
black they appeared blue. His eyes were just as
black and his skin as swarthy as a gypsy's. Feivel's
gabardine had perhaps a hundred rents in it reveal-
ing the lining beneath. His toes stuck out of his
boots. Feivel was not only taller but much stronger
than I. He always carried a heavy stick torn from
a bush, ready to protect me. If some boy called me
names, like shlemiel, shmagega, and the like,
Feivel would chase after him and beat him.
Feivel was both my disciple and my bodyguard. He
never grew tired of hearing my outlandish words
and weird stories. At times, when I flew into a
temper, I abused him and I even gave him a shove

or a slap, but he never struck back. At the same time he waged a silent war with me—the rebelliousness of a slave against his master seethed within him . . .

I could talk while we walked, but when Feivel wanted to say something he had to stop. Before he could get anything out he first blinked his eyes a few times. Even as he praised me, he implied that I fabricated things that made no sense whatsoever. He would say, "Since you say it, it's probably so . . ." And his gypsy-like eyes flashed with mockery.

Our plan to publish a book had gone awry, but I had a dozen other plans that day: we would establish a yeshiva for the secret study of the cabala. I would be the rabbi and he, Feivel, would be my beadle. I would become a heretic, and while I rode horseback on the Sabbath he, Feivel, would follow behind and listen to my wisdom. I would seal a covenant with Satan while he would bring the daughter of the Grand Vizier to me in my palace.

"What would you do with her?" Feivel asked me.

"Fly with her to the Mountains of Darkness."

"Oh, the things you say!"

"I fear no one . . ."

We crossed the Praga Bridge and our feet brought us of their own volition to the Terespol railroad station. I was drawn to trains. We went out on the platform. A train was about to depart for somewhere deep in Russia. The black locomotive belched smoke, hissed steam, and gushed hot water like some other-world beast. Its mighty driving wheel dripped oil. A huge gendarme—tall and broad, his face red and pockmarked, his deep chest hung with medals—paced to and fro issuing orders in Russian.

I said, "This train is going to Siberia."

"Where is Siberia?" Feivel asked.

"In the cold regions. The people there eat bear meat. For six months—the whole winter—it's night."

"When is it the Sabbath?" Feivel asked.

"There are no Jews there. It's never the Sabbath . . ."

"What's beyond Siberia?" Feivel asked.

"That's the end of the world. Giants live there who have three eyes in the center of their bellies."

"What do they eat"

"Each other . . ."

IV

In the evening I came home tired and sweaty. I hadn't eaten any lunch. My boots were dusty. My mother angrily brought me a mirror to show me how grimy my face was. She asked me again and

again where I had been all day, but I couldn't tell
her. In the living room, the ceiling lamp was lit.
We had a guest from Bilgoray, a man who traveled
around collecting subscriptions for the author of
a holy book. His name was Wolf Bear, but he
looked like a goat with his narrow white beard and
red-rimmed eyes. When he spoke, he moved his
gums like a goat chewing its cud. He wore a
patched gabardine and a soiled shirt with a
wrinkled collar. He had eaten supper at our house
and he conversed in a bleating voice. My older
brother, Joshua, also sat at the table as did my
sister, Hindele. Mother gave me what was left over
from both the meals I had missed—potatoes with
rice, dumplings with soup, a roast chicken liver,
and a slice of bread.

I was so hungry that I bolted down whole mouth-
fuls of food, while at the same time I pricked up
my ears to hear Wolf Bear's words. I heard him
say: "You become depressed when you travel
around, but you get to see the world. Every town
presents a different face. The people of Zelechow
are just as vicious as in the days when they drove
out Rabbi Levi Yitzchok in an ox wagon. In other
places they gave me the few gulden without any
questions, but in Zelechow they wanted to know
who the author was and demanded to see the
manuscript. They sat me down and began to argue
with me just as if I were the author. They also
found errors in the text. The women there all use

too much salt and pepper. They serve you a tiny morsel of meat and a lot of mustard. They eat rice pudding with horseradish. Everything there is done with sharpness. I go to a cobbler and ask if he can put half-soles on my boots, so what does he say? 'Why half-soles? Why not full soles? And why do you have to mention your boots? Where else would I put the soles, on your skullcap?' His eyes are piercing as a hedgehog's. They're all like that there, even the rabbi. You'll laugh, but in no other town do so many thorns grow as in Zelechow.

"How far is Zichlin from Zelechow? Not far. But the people there are as soft as silk. I come to the rabbi and show him the manuscript and he says, 'Thank God, holy books are still being written in this world. Jews don't forget the Torah.' In Zichlin the rabbi's wife herself made up a bed for me. They put honey on the table every day of the week. In Zelechow it's hard to arrange a match. All the girls become old maids. The young men go off to America and are never heard from again. I spent eight days in Zichlin and there was a wedding held each day. What's the sense behind this, eh? On the other hand, why did Sodom become Sodom? One leprous sheep infects the whole flock. It starts with one vicious person and it spreads to all. How did Warsaw become Warsaw? First they built one house, then another, and gradually a city emerged. Everything grows. Even stones grow."

"Stones don't grow, Reb Wolf Bear," my brother, Joshua, interjected.

"No? Well, so be it. There is a town in Volhynia called Maciejow where the sand is so deep that, when you fall into it, you can't get out. You sink down slowly. They say that if you put your ear to the sand, you can hear the cries of those trapped below. How can this be? How long can a person live underground, unless it's a doorway to Gehenna? On the road, I met a man from the Land of Israel. He spoke Hebrew. Aramaic too. He has seen the whole world. At first he said that he didn't know any Yiddish, but as we got to talking I saw that he did know it. He had visited Shushan, the old capital of Persia. He had been to Mount Ararat and seen Noah's ark. It rests on the tip of the mountain and eagles soar above it. You try to reach it because it seems so close, but when you get to the top, there is no ark. And that's how it is with all things. Illusion or who knows what. In what connection do I say this, eh? Yes, now I remember. The man was riding in the desert and he came to a place that was the gateway to Gehenna. You could hear the cries of the sinners. The earth is hollow there. There are caves underneath and cities and who knows what else."

"The earth isn't hollow," my brother, Joshua, said.

"Why not? Everything is possible. If you sit in one spot you think it's the same all over, but when you travel, you get to see all kinds of wonders. I've been to Wieliczka. They dig for salt there. There is enough salt for the whole world. They made houses out of salt, beds, even a wardrobe. In Czestochowa again, a statue of the Virgin Mary stands on a mountain. She is completely of gold and her eyes are diamonds. One time a man stole one of the eyes and replaced it with a glass one. He was caught in the act and sentenced to hard labor."

"Yes, I know, Macuch," I piped up.

"Eh? How do you know?" Reb Wolf Bear asked me.

"It was in the paper," I replied.

"Oh so? In olden times children knew nothing. Today they know everything. In Lublin there was a wonder child, a Yenuka, and at the age of three he sprouted a beard. At five he held a sermon in the synagogue and scholars came to debate with him. He was married at seven. When he reached nine, his beard turned as white as snow. He died at ten, an old man."

"Did you see this Yenuka with your own eyes?" Joshua asked.

"See him? No. But the whole world knows about it."

My father arched the brows over his blue eyes and his red beard glowed like gold. "Joshua, don't contradict!"

"It isn't true," Joshua said. He turned pale and his blue eyes reflected scorn.

"Have you been everywhere and do you know the truth?" Father asked. "The world is full of wonders. We only know what goes on down here. Only God the Almighty knows what happens in the other spheres."

I didn't know the reason myself, but an urge to cry came over me. I barely contained my tears. I went to my parents' bedroom and lay down on the bed in the dark. I suddenly realized—without knowing how myself—that I was too young to write a book. My brother, Joshua, often mentioned the word "literature." He told Mother that each nation creates its own literature. "That which Reb Wolf Bear now related at the table has to be literature," I thought. "But how can a beggar from a small village create literature?"

It was all one great mystery. I wasn't asleep yet, but my brain had already begun to weave a dream. Each time I tried to grasp it, its threads dissolved. I lay in bed, and at the same time I rode that train to Siberia. I heard the clacking of the wheels, the whistle of the locomotive. I heard my mother open the door and mumble, "Dozed off, the poor boy."

A few minutes later, I really fell asleep. The fantastic dreams started, the wild adventures. All the fantasies of the day turned into nocturnal visions. That night I dreamed that I was Rabbi Joseph della Rinah. I uttered God's name and the daughter of the Grand Vizier came flying to me. She looked like a neighbor's daughter, Estherel, who lived in our house on the third floor. In the dream, I asked Estherel, "What shall we do?"

And she replied, "I'll become your bride."

I awoke frightened, drenched in sweat. I had often heard my brother and my sister talk of love. Suddenly it became clear to me that I loved Estherel. I had heard that novels were written about love and it occurred to me to name the girl in my book Estherel and that I could become Ben Zion, who saved her from the cannibal and married her. I decided that when I grew up I would write not just a storybook but a whole novel about Estherel and myself.

The MS READ-a-thon needs young readers!

Boys and girls between 6 and 14 can join the MS READ-a-thon and help find a cure for Multiple Sclerosis by reading books. And they get two rewards — the enjoyment of reading, and the great feeling that comes from helping others.

Parents and educators: For complete information call your local MS chapter, or call toll-free (800) 243-6000. Or mail the coupon below.

Kids can help, too!

Mail to:
National Multiple Sclerosis Society
205 East 42nd Street
New York, N.Y. 10017

I would like more information about the MS READ-a-thon and how it can work in my area.

Name_____
(please print)

Address_____

City_____State_____Zip_____

Organization_____

MS-10/77

A PUBLIC SERVICE MESSAGE FROM DELL PUBLISHING CO., INC.